W9-AYA-635

ANIMAL RESCUE CENTER

The Runaway Rabbit

ANIMAL MAGIC

ANIMAL
RESCUE CENTER

Other titles in the series:

ANIMAL
RESCUE CENTER

The
Runaway
Rabbit

by TINA NOLAN

tiger tales

This series is for my riding friend Shelley,
who cares about all animals.

tiger tales
5 River Road, Suite 128, Wilton, CT 06897
Published in the United States 2017
Originally published in Great Britain 2007
by Little Tiger Group
Text copyright © 2007, 2017 Jenny Oldfield
Interior illustrations copyright © 2017 Artful Doodlers
Cover illustration copyright © 2017 Anna Chernyshova
Images courtesy of www.shutterstock.com
ISBN-13: 978-1-68010-407-3
ISBN-10: 1-68010-407-1
Printed in China
STP/1000/0238/0918
All rights reserved
10 9 8 7 6 5 4 3 2

For more insight and activities, visit us at www.tigertalesbooks.com

Contents

ANIMAL MAGIC
RESCUE CENTER

🏠 HOME

🐾 ADOPT

✋ FRIENDS

MEET THE ANIMALS IN NEED OF A HOME!

FRANKIE

A lively young ferret who had a bad start in life. Frankie is now looking for a fun-loving, kind owner. Are you that person?

KIKI

How can anyone not love Kiki? She's a gentle, sweet-tempered German shepherd who never loses her cool.

JIMMY

This little guinea pig's twinkling eyes will win you over and you'll long to take him home. Just look at his picture and fall in love!

SITE SEARCH 🔍

📰 **NEWS**

✋ **HELP US**

📞 **CONTACT**

🐾$ **DONATE!**

SHADOW

A Labrador and
border collie mix,
6 weeks old.
Email us fast or
she'll be gone!

BUDDY

This lively 2-year-
old boxer is bored!
He needs more
long walks and
a lot of TLC.

LUCKY

A beautiful black-
and-white Dutch
rabbit who is
lonely and looking
for a friend.

Chapter One
New Arrivals

"But this is a puppy. She's a living breathing creature—not a machine!" Mom told the woman at the reception desk at Animal Magic.

The visitor had marched in a few minutes earlier carrying a cardboard box containing a tiny black puppy.

Ella Harrison sat at the computer, surprised by her mom's angry tone.

"They told me at the place where I bought her that this puppy was house-trained," the woman complained in a whining voice. "But when I got her home, she started leaving puddles everywhere!"

"That's because Shadow is only about six weeks old," Mom explained more patiently. "It's much too soon for her to be house-trained."

The woman frowned. She was fashionably dressed in a short skirt and pink flowered top. "They also told me that she slept through the night and that she'd be perfectly happy to be left at home during the day while I go to work. But it's not true."

"You leave Shadow by herself *all* day?" Mom raised her eyebrows. She glanced at Ella, who made a face as she tapped at the keyboard to update the Animal

Magic website.

I don't believe it! Ella thought darkly.
Some people don't deserve pets!

Her mom took a deep breath. "Okay, let me get this straight. The breeders told you that Shadow was a purebred Labrador, but in fact she's a crossbreed—a mix of Labrador and collie by the look of it."

Ella turned to see the puppy raise her cute head over the top of the box and let out a faint whimper. *Poor little thing!*

"Plus, she's not house-trained. And she cries all night long?" Mom added.

The woman nodded three times. "So I don't want to keep her," she said firmly. "That's why I brought her here. After all, you are a rescue center, aren't you?"

"Crossbreeds are often very good-natured," Mom said quietly. "They can make better pets than pedigree dogs."

Definitely! Ella thought. *No way are crossbreeds second best!* But it was clear her mom was losing the argument.

"So will you take her or not?" the woman asked, tapping the side of the box and glancing at her watch.

Shadow whined and scratched with

her paws.

Mom succeeded in hiding her irritation. "Sure," she said brightly. "She's a beautiful little thing. It shouldn't take us long to find her a suitable new home."

Better than the one you gave her, Ella thought, glaring at the woman's pink flowery back as she turned to leave. Some people need a big reality check before they rush out and buy a pet!

As Mom showed the woman to the door, Ella came over and lifted the puppy out of the box and put her gently on the desk. "Hey, Shadow, she didn't even say good-bye to you, did she?" she muttered.

Shadow squirmed and yelped, her paws slipping on the smooth surface.

"Oops!" Ella smiled, lifting her carefully and cuddling her. "You're beautiful!" she said as the puppy snuggled close. Soft and silky, with big brown eyes and floppy ears, and a little pointed tail that wagged back and forth.

"It makes me so angry when people just dump off their pets!" Mom sighed, coming back into the reception area. "I'm also worried about that breeder passing off crossbreeds as pure pedigrees. I think it's worth following up."

Ella nodded as Shadow licked her hand. "You're totally beautiful!" she sighed. "You'll be snapped up the minute we put you up on our website—just wait and see!"

"Ella's in lo-ove!" Caleb chanted. "She lo-oves the new puppy because she's so cute and fluffy!"

"Who's cute and fluffy—Ella or the dog?" Ella and Caleb's dad asked, poking his head into the reception area.

Dad had just gotten home from a hot day delivering packages. He was in a good mood, ready to tease his daughter. "Or both?" he suggested.

Ella ignored the joke and continued putting flyers into the rack on the wall. "We admitted a new puppy named Shadow," she told him. "Caleb just took her picture and put her on the website."

"L-O-V-E—love!" Caleb laughed, unhooking a dog leash and going to get Buddy the boxer from the kennels. "I'm taking Buddy for a walk by the river," he told them.

The boxer jumped up when he saw Caleb's leash, wagging his stump of a tail.

"Down!" Caleb ordered. "Sit, Buddy!"

The lean brown dog did as he was told.

"Good boy." Caleb clipped on the leash

and took Buddy off across the yard.

"Nice dog," Dad said. "It's a shame about his habit of chewing people's shoes to shreds."

"And chair legs and tables," Ella reminded him. "But it's not Buddy's fault. His owner used to lock him in a room, and he was bored."

Buddy was a chewer and it had landed him at Animal Magic and in need of a new home. So far they'd had two sets of people come to look at the lively two year old, but both had turned him down because of his bad chewing habit.

"Hi, Ella. Hi, Mr. Harrison!" Annie Brooks said as she breezed in. Ella's friend from next door had come to see the puppy that Ella had called to tell her about. "So where's this cute puppy?"

"In the kennels. Come on!" Leaving the flyers, Ella dashed ahead. "Shadow's mega sweet, Annie. Honestly, you just have to take a peek!"

"Caleb's out walking Buddy, and Ella's in the kennels with Annie," Dad reported to Mom, who had just finished talking with Joel, Animal Magic's veterinary assistant.

"Did Annie bring any news?" Mom asked. "You know, from Linda—about the Council's decision."

For more than a week now they'd been waiting nervously for a letter from the Council.

"No news I'm afraid." Dad shook his head. "I only know that Linda wishes

she'd never filed that petition to have us closed down in the first place."

Mom frowned. "Yes, well, a dose of guilt won't do Linda Brooks any harm. Meanwhile, we're living on pins and needles, wondering whether we're going to be shut down."

Dad put an arm around her shoulder. "Fingers crossed they let us stay open," he said. "Anyway, forget that now. Come and see what's in the van!"

"Hey, go and see who we've got in the reception area!" Caleb told Ella and Annie.

The two girls had spent half an hour cuddling and petting little Shadow. Caleb was back from his walk and putting Buddy in his kennel.

"Who?" Ella demanded. It was early evening—a busy time for Animal Magic.

"Put that puppy down and go see!" Caleb insisted.

"Just because you want to cuddle Shadow!" Ella grinned.

"Yeah, Caleb!" Annie joined in. "You won't admit it, but really you do!"

"Okay then, don't go!" he sulked. "But you're missing something interesting."

"Here!" Ella said, making up her mind and handing Shadow to him. "Be careful that she doesn't have an accident all over you!"

Out in the reception area, Joel and Ella's mom and dad were gathered around a low table.

"Who's a silly boy?" a croaky voice asked. "Who's a silly boy?"

"What's that?" Annie gasped, tumbling through the door with Ella.

"Where's Neil? Who's a silly boy?" *Chirp-chirp-croak!*

"It's a bird," Ella decided, though she couldn't see clearly.

21

Dad leaned close to the cage and made little kissing noises. Joel's broad back hid the occupant from sight.

"Pep-py! Pep-py!" the voice croaked. "Who's a silly boy?"

Mom smiled. "Meet Peppy the parakeet," she said.

Inside the cage was a small, sky-blue bird with a white head and a gray freckled ruff of feathers around his neck. He hopped up and down on his little perch, bobbing his head and repeating his favorite phrase.

"Ohh!" Annie said with a sigh. "He's cute!"

The parakeet hopped from one perch to another, jingling a tiny silver bell above his head. "Who's a silly boy?" he cried, cocking his head to one side.

Ella crouched by the cage. She gazed into Peppy's button-black eyes. "Cool!" she muttered.

Peppy stared back at her without blinking. "Where's Neil?" he croaked. "Poppety-poppety-poppety-pop!"

Chapter Two

The Shy Rabbit

"Who's Neil?" Ella asked her dad the
following morning.

Peppy the parakeet had been going on
about Neil ever since he arrived.

"Neil is Peppy's owner," Dad
explained. "He left the bird with us
while he goes on vacation to see his
sister in London. He'll be back in three
weeks."

"Cool!" Ella grinned. She laughed
as Peppy hopped and poppety-popped
like crazy in his cage. The talking

bird's bright eyes and tiny sharp claws
fascinated her.

"Any mail this morning?" Mom asked
as she dashed through the reception
area.

"Not yet," Ella answered.

"I can't stand this waiting around,"
her mom sighed. "It's driving me crazy!"

For a while there was a stiff silence.
Then Dad abruptly changed the
subject. "How's little Shadow?"

"Good," Ella said with a smile. She'd
checked the cute puppy twice already.
"Hey, Dad, why aren't you at work?"

"Day off. And why aren't you at
school, Ella-Bella?"

"Summer vacation!" she told him. "As
if you didn't know! And what's with the
baby name stuff?"

As they joked around, the main door opened and a tall, fair-haired man and a girl around six years old came in. They glanced around uncertainly, then walked to the desk.

"Can I help you?" Dad asked.

Ella noted the small blue pet carrier under the man's arm.

"My name is Fred Nichols, and this is my daughter, Paige. We hope we've come to the right place," the man began.

The little girl looked down at her feet with an unhappy frown.

"This is Animal Magic, where we match the perfect pet with the perfect owner!" Dad announced with a smile. "At least, that's what we try to do."

Mr. Nichols cleared his throat. "Good. Well, I mean, in one way, it's good. But in another way it's not good, is it, Paige?"

The girl shook her head.

"We're very sorry to part with Beanie," her dad went on. He placed the pet carrier on the desk and stood Paige on a nearby chair. "But we're going abroad, so we don't have any choice."

Intrigued, Ella came over to investigate.

"How long will you be away?" Dad asked, thinking that the parting might not be forever.

"Oh, we're not coming back," Mr. Nichols explained. "We're moving to Canada. That's why we have to say good-bye to Beanie."

"So who's Beanie?" Ella asked, unzipping the carrier and peering inside.

At first she saw only a soft, pale-blue blanket. Then, looking more closely, she made out a white shape huddled among the folds. It was round and furry, with long ears and enormous dark brown eyes. "A baby rabbit!" she muttered, reaching inside.

But Beanie didn't want to be picked up. She turned her back and shrank further into the corner.

"Beanie's very shy," Paige's dad explained. "We've only had her for a couple of weeks and we've not been able to coax her out of her shell, I'm afraid."

For the first time Paige spoke up. "She only lets *me* pet her," she said quietly. "No one else."

Gently the little girl put her hand inside the carrier and petted Beanie's ears.

"Does she eat food from your hand?" Ella asked.

Paige nodded. "She likes lettuce and tiny bits of carrot."

"How come you took Beanie in?" Dad asked Mr. Nichols.

"When we already knew we were moving, you mean?"

Dad nodded.

"It was a case of us or nobody, I'm

afraid. We found Beanie in our shed. She was obviously lost. We figured she'd given her previous owners the slip, so we took her in. My wife put up 'Found' notices around the neighborhood, but no one came forward to claim her."

Dad nodded and began to take down details. Meanwhile, Paige showed Ella how to pet Beanie.

"You put your hand in front of her, like this. You wait for her to sniff. If she likes you, she'll let you move your hand a bit closer, until in the end she lets you pet her."

Patiently Ella copied Paige. "Poor little Beanie!" she sighed. "Don't be shy. I'm not going to hurt you."

The small white rabbit trembled as she sniffed Ella's hand. But she no longer tried to hide in the corner. Instead, she

came forward just a little bit.

"Pretty girl!" Ella soothed. "You're beautiful, with your big, brown eyes."

Paige nodded and smiled.

Sniff-sniff. Beanie's ears twitched as she edged forward.

In the background, Peppy jingled his bell and poppety-popped.

"We live at 23 Ridgewood Lane," Mr. Nichols told Dad, as he filled out the form. "But we're leaving first thing tomorrow."

"Okay, thanks. I'm sure we'll be able to find Beanie a new owner," Dad said, smiling kindly at Paige as her dad helped her down from the chair. "And once she's settled in to her new home, we could send you a message to tell you how happy she is. Would you like us to do that?"

Paige frowned then nodded.

"So we'll email you with the good news. Is that okay?"

Another nod, then Paige blinked back a tear.

"Come on, Paige, let's go," her dad said briskly. He took her hand. "Say good-bye."

"Good-bye, Beanie," Paige whispered as her dad led her away.

Inside the pet carrier, hidden from sight, shy Beanie snuggled deep into the blue blanket.

"Where's Neil? Who's a silly boy?" Peppy chattered from his perch.

"Let me give you a guided tour of Animal Magic!" Ella said to Beanie.

Her mom had checked the baby rabbit and declared her fit. "Very nervous, though," she'd warned. "It'll take a while for her to get used to us."

Ella picked up the blue carrier with Beanie inside and made her way to the cat area, which was nice and quiet. "I'm going to read about rabbit care," she promised, placing the carrier next to a kitten unit and peering in at Beanie. "I know you need plenty of clean water to drink, but I want to find out more stuff about a healthy diet and exercise."

Beanie sat cozily on her blanket, her white fur fluffy, her ears long and silky.

"This is where we take care of cats and kittens," Ella explained, pointing down the row of units. "We've got Benny and Domino. Domino is the black-and-white

cat. We've already found a home for
him. These two kittens are named Missy
and Petal."

Even though she didn't venture out
of her cozy nest, Beanie seemed to be
paying attention. Her nose twitched,
and she flicked her long ears.

"Insane!" Caleb muttered as he passed
through the cat area. "Crazy girl Ella,
talking to the animals!"

"And that's my brother, Caleb," Ella
told Beanie. "Ignore everything he says,
okay?"

Ella showed Beanie the kennels with
the noisy dogs, including Buddy the
bad-boy boxer and Kiki, a calm, sweet-
tempered German shepherd.

But shy Beanie hid in her dark corner, afraid of the barks and yelps.

So Ella quickly carried her out of the kennels to the small pets section.

"Meet Jimmy," she said to the quivering newcomer. "He's a handsome brown and white guinea pig with twinkly pink eyes. And this is Frankie the ferret, who was dumped in a pet shop doorway. He was practically starving. How can people do that? And next to him is Lucky, a Dutch rabbit. I'm sure you'll soon make friends with him."

"Nuts!" Caleb commented, coming in to play with Frankie. He took the ferret from his cage and let him run up his arm onto his shoulder. "Talk, talk, talk to the animals. That's all Ella ever does!"

As usual, Ella ignored her brother and continued her guided tour.

"We have new stables out in the yard. At the moment we don't have anyone living there because it's summer and Buttercup and Chance stay out in Mrs. Brooks's field at the back of their house, which is next door."

Beanie sniffed the air and edged forward to the door of the carrier. She stared out at her new surroundings.

Frankie ran down Caleb's other arm and jumped onto the table beside Beanie. A startled Beanie cowered back in her dark corner.

"Hey, Frankie, don't scare her!" Ella protested. She knew the ferret was too lively for the shy rabbit. So, with a fresh idea in her head, Ella ran to the kennels to get Shadow.

"Now, Shadow, meet Beanie. I want you to be nice to Beanie. She's new and she needs a friend. I'm relying on you!" Ella introduced the gentle puppy to the young rabbit.

Shadow poked her nose into the carrier and wagged her tail.

"Uh?" Caleb quizzed, as Frankie sprinted up and down his arm. "A dog and a rabbit? That's not a good idea."

"Why not?" Ella asked.

"Dog and rabbit together. Dog chases rabbit. Rabbit ends up seriously dead!"

"Not this time." Ella grinned as Shadow made friendly moves toward Beanie. "Beanie isn't scared—look!"

The white rabbit twitched her ears and sniffed. Her big brown eyes gleamed.

Caleb shrugged. "Do what you like," he mumbled. "You always do, anyway."

"They're going to be best friends," Ella promised.

As if to prove it, Shadow crept in beside Beanie and snuggled down in the blue blanket.

Things were looking up. Poor abandoned Shadow was happy. Shy Beanie had found a friend.

But even as Ella leaned in and petted them both, a small worry formed inside her head.

Why did Beanie show up in the Nichols' shed in the first place?

"Where did you come from, you sweet little thing?" she muttered, tickling Beanie's ears. "Were you naughty? Did you run away?"

Beanie stared up at Ella with her huge, dark eyes.

"Is someone out there still missing you?" Ella wondered aloud. "And if so, how do we find them and take you home?"

Chapter Three
Puppy Walking

"Okay, so *where* is this letter from
the Council?" Mom sighed. She sifted
through the mail on the desk in the
reception area, checking for the third
time to see if the letter had arrived.

Joel helped her, while Ella watched
Caleb enter Beanie's details onto the
Animal Magic website.

"Beanie. Young white rabbit, looking
for a friend. Owners have moved away."
Caleb typed fast, then uploaded a

picture he had taken with his phone. "Is this one okay?" he asked Ella, showing her a close-up of Beanie.

She nodded. "So-o cute!"

"I spoke to the man from the Council, Mr. Winters, and he insists he sent the letter containing their decision on Monday," Mom went on. "Of course, he won't tell me what it is over the phone...."

"Is this it?" Joel asked, unearthing a crumpled brown envelope. "Oh, no, it's a bill from the lumber yard—for the wood we used to build the stables."

"Don't remind me," Mom groaned. "It came last month, and I still haven't paid it. I'm not likely to be able to find the extra money this month, either."

Luckily for Ella, Annie showed up before she got dragged into the search

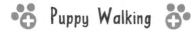

for the Council letter.

"Hey, Ella, when can we take Shadow out?" Annie asked brightly.

"Right now!" Ella jumped at the chance. "Come on! We can start training her, too!"

It was a bright, sunny afternoon, and Ella soon forgot the big question regarding the future of Animal Magic.

"The grass is taller than Shadow!" Ella cried as the black puppy scampered through the safely-fenced field at the back of Annie's house. "You can just see the tip of her tail."

Shadow zigzagged through the pink meadow flowers. At the bottom of the field, Buttercup and Chance grazed quietly.

43

"Call Shadow back," Annie told Ella. "See if she obeys."

"Here, Shadow!" Ella called.

The puppy romped on, bounding over clumps of buttercups, heading for two women who stood near the horses.

"That's Mom and Miss Elliot. Miss Elliot called to see Buttercup," Annie reported.

"Here, Shadow!" Ella called more sternly.

Still the puppy scampered on until she reached the horses.

"Oops!" Ella cried, as Buttercup lowered her head and snorted loudly.

Shadow yelped and fled to Mrs. Brooks for protection. *Save me from that fierce giant with hot breath and enormous hooves!*

Mrs. Brooks picked Shadow up and waited for the girls to join them.

"I'm sorry, Mrs. Brooks. The training isn't going so well!" Ella gasped. "Shadow wouldn't obey my command."

"But she's a cute little thing," Miss Elliot said, reaching out to pet her.

"Hello, Miss Elliot." Ella smiled at Buttercup's ex-owner. "Isn't Chance doing well?"

Miss Elliot nodded. "It's wonderful to see Buttercup being such a good mother to him. And how are your mother and father doing with their animal rescue work?"

"Good, thanks," Ella said, carefully avoiding Mrs. Brooks's gaze as she took Shadow from her. After all, the only cloud on the horizon—the petition to

have Animal Magic closed down—had
been caused by their next-door neighbor.

Mrs. Brooks blushed but said nothing.

"Come and see us anytime you like!"
Ella invited.

"I will," Miss Elliot promised with a
sweet smile. "In fact, I'd like that very
much."

Ella left Annie with her mom and Miss
Elliot and ran back home with Shadow.
Mom, Dad, and Joel were still searching
high and low for the letter from the
Council.

"It must be here somewhere," Mom
muttered, down on her hands and knees,
looking under the rack full of flyers. "It
must have been delivered by now."

Ella carried Shadow into the small pets section. "What are you doing?" she asked Caleb, who was searching inside Jimmy the guinea pig's cage. "Are you still looking for the letter, or did Frankie take off again?"

He shook his head and looked worried. "I let Frankie meet Beanie—you know, like you did with Shadow—and everything was okay, they were getting along fine, until I turned my back—just for a second, to get Frankie's food out of the fridge—and when I looked again, well, Beanie had vanished!"

"Beanie!" Ella echoed. "Where? I mean, how…?"

"I don't know, but she couldn't have gone far," Caleb groaned, peering into Lucky the rabbit's cage. "Ella, we've

48

got to find Beanie before Mom finds out. Come on, put Shadow back in her kennel and help me look!"

Chapter Four
Hide-and-seek

Caleb and Ella searched every corner of the small pets section.

Ella looked under shelves and inside cupboards. Caleb took each animal out of its cage and searched around in its bedding.

"Any sign?" he asked Ella.

She shook her head. "Mr. Nichols told us Beanie was really timid and that she runs away if anything scares her. I bet that's how she ended up in their shed in

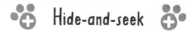

the first place."

"Maybe we should try tempting her with some food," Caleb suggested.

Ella nodded. "I'll go grab a lettuce leaf."

She opened the fridge door and reached for the lettuce. "Oh!" she gasped, quickly shutting it again. "Caleb, I found Beanie!"

Her brother came running. "In the fridge?" he asked.

Ella nodded. "In the vegetable drawer. She must have snuck in there when you opened the door."

"Phew! Crisis over," Caleb said, relieved.

"Yes, but she's going to freeze if she stays in there much longer."

"Yeah, sorry." Caleb bit his lip.

"How are we going to get her out?" Ella asked. "If I open the door again, she could jump out and run off. Then we'd be back to where we started."

"I'll go get her blue blanket," Caleb decided. "Wait until I've draped it over the front of the fridge, then open the door again. Beanie will probably shoot out but the blanket will be blocking her exit and I'll bundle her up in it. Okay?"

Ella nodded. "It might work," she muttered. In any case, they had to get Beanie out of there fast. "Let's give it a try."

Waiting for Caleb to get the blanket in position, Ella eased open the fridge door. For a few seconds nothing happened. Then they heard a scratching sound and saw a bump in the blanket as Beanie made her attempt at freedom.

In a flash Caleb let one edge of the

blanket drop to trap the baby rabbit
inside it. Then Ella picked up the bundle
and carried it to Beanie's pet carrier.

"Good job, Ella!" Caleb muttered,
very relieved.

Gently Ella released the captive rabbit. Beanie sat safe in her carrier, shivering and blinking up at them. "Don't worry, we'll get a proper cage ready for you," Ella told her, "with cozy bedding and a dish of yummy food."

Beanie twitched her long ears and cowered in the corner.

"You can't keep on running away like this," Ella scolded. "You have to learn to let us take care of you. After all, it's a big, dangerous world out there for a baby rabbit!"

Beanie blinked and seemed to sigh.

"She probably runs away because she's scared," Caleb pointed out. "Anyway, I'm going to take Buddy for a walk. Let's hope I'm safer with dogs than I am with rabbits!"

"And I'll fix up a cage for Beanie," Ella said.

She didn't give Caleb a hard time. After all, Beanie was back, and that was all that mattered.

"It isn't my day!" Caleb said, reappearing five minutes later with Buddy the bad-boy boxer. "We didn't get further than the reception area."

"What happened?" Ella asked.

She'd found a cage for Beanie and finished feeding her. Now she was checking on Jimmy, Lucky, and Frankie.

"Buddy's been up to his tricks again," Caleb groaned. "Anyway, Mom and Dad want you to come over to the house."

Ella washed her hands at the sink.

"So what's Buddy done this time?" she asked Caleb as they dashed through the

reception area.

"Poppety-poppety-pop!" Peppy croaked. "Where's Neil? Who's a silly boy?"

Caleb grimaced. "When we got out front, Mom and Dad were still looking for that letter."

"From the Council," Ella nodded. "So?"

"So Buddy pulls on his leash and drags me to the bench in the waiting area and starts sniffing around underneath it...."

"Don't tell me!" Ella gasped.

Caleb nodded. "Underneath is a pile of well-chewed mail, including the letter from the Council. Buddy must have somehow snuck the letters out of the pile of mail without anyone seeing him—maybe yesterday or the day before! He mangled it and dumped it under the bench!"

Ella gave a low whistle.

"So now he remembers where he stashed it, and he goes back and chews it some more—right in front of our eyes!"

"One munched-up piece of precious mail!" Ella gasped.

"Dad managed to rescue the letter before Buddy wrecked it completely. They've taken it over to the house.

They're waiting for me to get you before they open it."

Ella held her breath as they crossed the yard and entered the kitchen. She crossed her fingers, staring at the chewed letter, which her mom held in her hands.

"Can I open it now?" Mom asked Dad. He nodded.

"Let's hope we get the decision we want!" Mom muttered, opening the letter with trembling fingers.

Chapter Five
Good News

"'Dear Mrs. Harrison,'" Mom read slowly.

The edges of the paper were torn and chewed, the middle was scrunched and crumpled.

"'With regard to the matter of the petition raised and presented to the Council by Mrs. Linda Brooks of Main Street, Crystal Park....'"

"It's all down to Mrs. Brooks!" Ella muttered to Caleb. "None of this would ever have happened if it hadn't been for her!"

"Shhh!" Dad warned, before Mom read on.

"'After due consideration of all the factors including noise nuisance and frequent traffic access from Main Street into Animal Magic, the Council has decided…'"

"Please, please, please let us stay open!" Ella said softly, her fingers crossed.

Mom took a breath and glanced up at Dad, "'…to grant permission for the animal rescue center to remain *open* and to continue its work.'"

"Yes!" Caleb jumped up and punched the air. "We can carry on."

"Yes!" Ella sank onto a chair and heaved the biggest sigh of relief. "I

can't wait to tell Annie the good news.
Hey, can we have a party to celebrate?
Please say yes!"

"Good idea," Dad agreed.

He hugged Mom, who allowed herself
10 seconds of glad tears, then pulled
herself together.

"Sure, we can stay open and that's a big relief," she said. "But at the rate we're going with debts and everything, we're definitely going to have to cut back on some things. Anyway, it's six o'clock—time to feed the dogs," she told Caleb. "Ella, will you clean out Peppy's cage, then deal with the small animals?"

Ella and Caleb nodded and shot out of the house as fast as their legs would carry them.

"Hey, Buddy, you sneaky letter-gobbler—you're in big trouble!" Caleb warned the boxer.

Buddy jumped up and licked Caleb's neck. Then he ran to his bowl and began to wolf down his supper.

"He is," Caleb insisted to Shadow, who dashed to her kennel door wagging her tiny black tail. "We need to stop him from eating everything in sight if we're going to find him a new owner."

Shadow yelped and jumped up at Caleb as he brought her bowl.

In his kennel next door, Buddy licked the bowl clean.

"Buddy's in trouble," Ella told Peppy. She took out the soiled lining from the bottom of his cage and replaced it with a new one.

"Poppety-pop!" Peppy squawked, staring down at Ella's busy hands.

"But I expect Mom won't be too hard on him," Ella explained. "The Council said yes to Animal Magic, so she'll be in a mega-good mood! We can stay open, we can stay open!" she trilled. "And Dad says maybe we can have a big party!"

Peppy watched Ella pour seed into his plastic bowl. Fluttering down from his perch, he dipped his head into the bowl and cracked a seed between his beak.

"Of course, we need more kennels," Ella went on happily. She closed the cage door and checked the latch. "We don't have nearly enough space for all the dogs and cats that are brought here."

Going through to the small animals, she chattered on. "Hi, Jimmy, hi, Frankie. Did you hear? The Council will let us stay open!"

Frankie the ferret dived into his deep bed of straw and wood shavings. Jimmy's pink eyes twinkled as he shuffled slowly across his cage.

"Hey, Beanie!" Ella said gently to the little white rabbit. "We just got the best news. Animal Magic can stay open. We can keep matching the perfect pet with the perfect owner!"

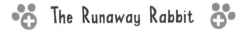

Pausing for a moment, Ella gazed at the shy, runaway rabbit. "Don't be scared," she whispered. "We won't send you to a bad home."

Beanie twitched her ears and huddled in a tighter ball.

"I promise," Ella insisted, crouching low and meeting Beanie's wide, dark gaze. "We'll find someone who loves you and who will take care of you really well and will never scare you or make you run away ever again!"

Chapter Six
Ella's Promise

"Where are we going?" Annie asked
Ella.

The two girls rode their bikes along
Main Street early on Thursday morning.
It was a gray, cloudy day. There were
puddles in the road.

"Yuck!" Ella cried as a red car
overtook them and splashed her. "I
already had my shower this morning,
thank you!"

Annie laughed. "So?" she asked.

"Where are you dragging me off to this time?"

Ella rode ahead, turning right at the top of the main road and heading toward the river. "I have an idea," was all she would say.

"Where's Ella?" Mom asked Caleb.

Caleb was hunched over the computer, trying to set up a visit for Buddy. A man named John Smith had emailed to say he might be interested in offering him a home.

"Caleb, where did Ella go?" Mom repeated.

"She went out on her bike with Annie," Caleb answered.

"Did she say where?"

Caleb tapped at the keyboard. "Dunno. She said something about Ridgewood Lane. I'm not sure why."

"What's the big mystery?" Annie insisted as she and Ella leaned their bikes against a bench overlooking the river.

Ella sat her friend down on the bench and talked earnestly. "Well, I've been thinking a lot about Beanie and how shy and nervous she is. She really, really needs a kind owner."

"Not just any stranger who walks into Animal Magic looking for a pet rabbit," Annie agreed.

"I promised I'd find someone who loves her and won't scare her," Ella said.

69

Annie nodded. "But that still doesn't explain why you dragged me here."

Ella pointed to the row of houses behind them. "This is Ridgewood Lane. The house with the moving van outside is number 23. That's where Paige Nichols lives."

Annie frowned. "But you told me they were moving. That's why Paige had to leave Beanie with you."

As the two girls talked, men came and went out of number 23. They carried big boxes into the van.

"It is," Ella went on. "But Paige cares a lot about Beanie. That's why she'll try to help us find the first owners."

"You mean the owners before the Nichols family?" Annie asked.

"Yes, it just came to me in a flash. We have to find them—trace the clues, track them down—so we can give Beanie back to her owners!"

"I don't get it," Annie said. "From what you told me, they didn't even bother to try and find her when she ran away."

"Maybe they did, maybe they didn't," Ella argued. "But just because Beanie ran off and got lost in the shed, it doesn't mean her owners didn't love her." Leave it to Annie to squash her great idea!

"But Paige's mom put up notices everywhere."

"I know. But maybe the owners were away on vacation at the time and never saw them. Who knows?"

As they sat and thought it through, Ella spotted the small, fair-haired figure of Paige Nichols standing at the gate of number 23. Ella waved and then ran to join her.

"How's Beanie?" Paige wanted to know the moment she saw Ella.

"She's fine. She's got a big, comfy cage at Animal Magic. She's nice and warm and she's eating a lot."

Paige nodded slowly. "Is she sad?" she asked, tears welling up in her big gray eyes. "Does she miss me?"

"A little bit," Ella admitted. "But she'll soon settle down. Anyway, I wanted to ask you some more questions about when you found Beanie in your shed. Is that okay?"

Slowly Paige nodded, then led Ella into her yard. Annie waited by the moving van.

"Can I see the shed?" Ella asked Paige. "And can you tell me what happened on the day you found Beanie?"

"It was busy. We had a lot of people looking around the house," Paige explained as she took Ella to the shed.

"So when did you find Beanie?" she asked.

"After everyone had left. It was quiet, and I was playing by myself in the yard."

"Was the shed door open?"

Paige nodded. "I was playing soccer and I kicked my ball inside by mistake. I was looking for it under the shelf with all the flowerpots, and that's when I found her."

"Was she hiding?"

"Yes. Some flowerpots had fallen off the shelf and rolled into a corner. Beanie was hiding inside one. She was so scared that she was shaking all over."

"I would be, too," Ella said quietly. "If I was Beanie and I was lost in a big, strange yard with tall trees and dark bushes, I'd be scared stiff. So what did you do?"

"I shut the door, then sat down and talked to her," Paige explained. "I didn't try to pick her up because I didn't want to scare her any more."

Ella smiled at Paige's sweet and serious face. "Then what?"

"After a little while, Beanie stopped shivering. She let me pet her. Then Dad came out looking for me and I asked him to come in and close the shed door. It was Dad who picked Beanie up and took her into the house."

"Did she struggle?"

"Yes. She tried to run away from Dad."

"She does that a lot," Ella admitted. "And after that you took care of Beanie and she let you be her friend?"

"Yes, and I didn't want to bring her to Animal Magic," Paige sniffed. "I wanted to keep her! But Dad said it was the only thing to do."

The noise of men shifting furniture inside the house reached them, and Ella saw how sad Paige was about leaving Beanie. "Beanie will be okay, I promise," she told her quietly. "Can I tell you what I'm planning to do?"

Paige nodded, and she wiped a tear from her cheek.

"I want to find the people who lost Beanie in the first place. I think they must be sad about her running away, and I'm sure they must want her back."

"Are you sure?" Paige whispered. Like Annie, she remembered the notices her mom had put up, and how no one had replied.

"Absolutely!" Ella said with a bright smile. "And when I find her real owners, I'll email and tell you. I'll even send you a pretty picture of Beanie with her family, back where she belongs!"

Chapter Seven
Billy's Bad Habit

"My mom says you should never make promises you can't keep," Annie told Ella.

All the way back home from Ridgewood Lane, Annie had been grumbling about Ella's idea.

"Who says I can't keep my promise?" Ella retorted. "I don't think it will be too hard to track down Beanie's owner."

"And if your plan works, what then?" At the gate of Animal Magic,

Annie braked, then got off her bike.
"Like I said—I really don't think the
people who lost Beanie care about her.
Otherwise, they'd have tried really hard
to find her after she ran away."

Ella got off her bike and looked Annie
in the eye. "Sometimes you're so…"

"…So?"

"…So *annoying*!" Ella replied,
flouncing off across the yard.

"Buddy's really friendly and good-natured," Caleb was telling John Smith in the reception area.

John had driven out to Animal Magic especially to see the boxer. He nodded and petted the dog, who wriggled his backside and wagged his tail.

"He likes you," Caleb said.

Behind the desk, Mom and Joel worked at the computer, updating their records.

"I had a boxer named Bruno when I was a kid," John told them. "I've always liked this breed."

"Then you know they need plenty of exercise," Mom warned.

Caleb frowned. He could see that John and Buddy were bonding like crazy and secretly hoped that his mom wouldn't come out with the stuff about Buddy's bad chewing habit.

"I don't mind that," John said. "Walking Buddy would get me out of the house. But how come he ended up here with you?"

"His previous owners had little kids. They couldn't cope," Caleb said vaguely. Out of the corner of his eye he saw Ella flounce through the main door and head straight for one of the computers.

"Actually, Buddy has one very bad habit," Mom told John.

Uh-oh! Inwardly Caleb groaned. That was it—they might as well take an

ugly mug-shot of Buddy and put him permanently behind bars!

"He chews," Mom explained. "Shoes, furniture—anything he can get his teeth into. We have to warn you in advance, because there would be no point in you taking him home and finding out the hard way."

"Oh, yeah, I remember Bruno used to do that," John said, thoughtfully patting Buddy's broad head. "He wrecked three pairs of my dad's slippers, but my mom cured him in the end."

"How?" Caleb asked quickly.

John shook his head. "Don't know. I can't remember. I'll have to ask Mom."

"Well, we'd love to know how to cure him," Mom said, smiling.

John nodded. "But now that you've

told me about this, I'll definitely need
a day or two to think about adopting
Buddy. And I need to discuss it with my
girlfriend—okay?"

"Fine," Mom agreed.

Not fine! Caleb thought. *It's back to the
kennels for you, Buddy boy!*

As he led Buddy out of the reception
area, he glanced over Ella's shoulders
and saw her tapping away at the
keyboard. "Do you know this rabbit?"
he read in large letters on the screen.
Underneath was a big photo of Beanie.
"What are you up to?" he mumbled.

"What does it look like? I'm making a
flyer."

Buddy had stopped and turned round
to see John leave the building without
looking back. He whined and sidled

close to Caleb.

"A flyer? What for?" Caleb asked.

"To put in people's mailboxes." Ella concentrated on her typing. "Beanie is a runaway rabbit who misses her owners. If you recognize her, please contact us."

"The Nichols already tried that," Caleb pointed out.

"No, they didn't. They only put up posters. They didn't deliver them to people's houses."

"Did you check with Mom and Dad?"

"Nope. But don't worry, they'll say it's a good idea." Ella was confident that her parents would back her up.

"Anyway, how do you know Beanie's first owners weren't cruel to her? Maybe that's why she ran away in the first place," Caleb pointed out.

Ella sighed. "Listen!" she said. "I don't know for sure, do I? But my guess is they were nice, kind people. They were just careless for a moment and let Beanie escape. Now they're really sad that she's missing."

"Says you!" Caleb retorted. He still wasn't convinced. "Anyway, putting flyers in mailboxes won't do any good."

"Be quiet, Caleb!" Ella snapped. She clicked the "print" key and waited for the flyers to roll out of the printer.

"We've got three inquiries from people interested in adopting Shadow," Mom reported to Ella when she came back from delivering Beanie flyers up and down Main Street.

"Cool," Ella muttered. She tweeted at Buddy in his cage behind the reception area, then placed her extra flyers on the desk.

"Do you want to help with a vaccination?" her mom asked, looking toward the entrance at a man and a boy with a small black-and-white

puppy. "Hello, Mr. Robinson, hello, Ben!" she called. "Come right this way."

Ella nodded and went into the hospital, where she cleaned the table with antiseptic spray. Then Ben and his dad brought the puppy in, and Mom followed.

"Thanks for fitting us in so quickly," Mr. Robinson told her. "I've been telling Ben that we can't take Buster for walks until he's been vaccinated."

"That's right," Mom nodded. "How old is Buster? About seven weeks?"

"Six and a half," Mr. Robinson confirmed. "We bought him from a dubious place, I'm afraid. The mother is a pure bred Lab, and the owners were trying to pass this little guy off as pure Labrador, too, but I could tell at a glance that he wasn't. My bet is that there's quite a bit of border collie in him, too."

Mom glanced at Ella. "Sounds like Buster comes from the same litter as Shadow—a crossbreed puppy who was brought in to us a couple of days ago.

I hope you didn't pay a pedigree price."

"No," Mr. Robinson replied, as Mom quickly gave Buster his jab and gave him back to Ben. "We're moving out to Crystal Park from the city, which is finally why we allowed Ben to have a puppy."

As her mom led Ben and his dad back into the reception area, Ella slipped off to see Beanie.

"I saw Paige," she told the rabbit, putting her nose against the front of Beanie's cage. "She's missing you a lot."

Beanie twitched her nose and took one short hop toward Ella.

"I'm going to put flyers about you in every mailbox in town," Ella went on. "I've already started on Main Street."

Another hop closer. Beanie seemed less

shy today, maybe drawn by the sound of Ella's gentle voice.

"This is good. You like me talking to you, don't you?" Ella said.

But suddenly Beanie's ears twitched and she shot back into the darkest corner. She'd caught sight of a face at the window.

Ella glanced around in time to see Ben Robinson peering in at them. He looked flushed, and his forehead was creased in a worried frown.

Thanks, Ben! Ella thought. *Just when I was getting to bond with Beanie, you have to go and startle her!*

Ben saw Ella watching him and quickly ducked out of sight.

Weird! Ella said to herself. *Why is he acting so strange?*

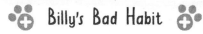

In the corner of her cage, Beanie sat huddled in a soft white ball, with only her big, dark eyes moving, watching for enemies and trying to hide.

"I'll come and talk to you later," Ella sighed. With shy Beanie, it was always one step forward and two steps back.

Chapter Eight
A Different Plan

Early the next morning, Ella went out to deliver more of her Beanie flyers.

"Good luck!" Dad shouted from his van as he set off for work. He and Ella had discussed her plan to find Beanie's real owner, and unlike Caleb, he'd thought the flyers were a good idea.

"Thanks, Dad!" Ella smiled and waved.

She headed down Main Street, turning onto Red Oak Drive and putting a flyer in the mailbox in front of each house. Back on Main Street, she came to Arbor Court, and wasn't surprised to see Miss Elliot standing at the door of her small house. She waved at the elderly lady and went across.

"Have you seen Tigger?" Miss Elliot asked.

Tigger was Miss Elliot's beloved tabby cat. Ella shook her head.

"I'm worried about the traffic. Tigger isn't used to it."

"Don't worry. I'll keep a lookout. Would you like one of these?" Ella showed Miss Elliot the flyer.

Miss Elliot nodded. "I hope you find the owner. She's such a sweet little rabbit, isn't she? Someone somewhere must be heartbroken about losing her."

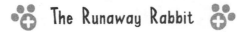

"That's exactly what I think!" Ella agreed.

"And how is your mother? And the rescue center?"

"Cool, actually. The Council says we can stay open, which is a great big weight off our shoulders. But it means Mom is mega-busy. Besides, she's worried about owing people money. But that shouldn't stop you from coming by to see us anytime you want, by the way," Ella continued. She liked Miss Elliot, but she was eager to get on her way.

"I need to bring Tigger in soon for his rabies shot," Miss Elliot said, relieved when she spotted the little tabby strolling across the lawn in the middle of the yard. "Here, Tigger!" she called and clapped her hands.

Seizing her chance, Ella hurried on. Soon she'd made it to the edge of town, so she crossed the road, turned onto a side street, and delivered her flyers to the big houses on Three Oaks Road.

"Hey, Ella!" Caleb's friend, George Stevens, was in his driveway, dressed in jeans and a blue T-shirt, his dark hair tousled as if he'd just crawled out of bed. "What do you have there?"

"Flyers." Ella blushed and tried to squeeze past him. Somehow George always made her feel about five years old. He acted like he was a grown-up, looking down at a scruffy kid.

"Let's see!" George stretched out his hand and grabbed a flyer. "Hmm, cute. Is this the rabbit Caleb told me about—the one that ran off and hid in the fridge?"

Ella nodded, her cheeks flushing deeper than ever.

"It just so happens that we have a spare rabbit cage and a run in our backyard," George went on. "I had pet rabbits when I was younger, but I haven't had one in a while. I like the look of Beanie, though."

"Uh-huh," Ella muttered. "But actually, Beanie's different. We're not trying to find a new home for her right now."

"Are you sure? Caleb said he'd put her on the website."

Ella swallowed hard. "Yeah, but look at the flyer. It says that we're searching for Beanie's owner."

"That's not what Caleb told me." George frowned. "I bet if I went down to Animal Magic right now and offered five-star rabbit accommodations with a big cage and a long run out the back, your mom would jump at the chance!"

"I don't think so." Ella shook her head. "That's not the plan for Beanie."

But the more she argued, and the longer George looked at Beanie's cute photo, the less he seemed to be listening.

"In fact, I think I'll ride down there right now," George decided, disappearing inside the garage to grab his bike.

"No—wait!" Ella said feebly. She had to step quickly out of George's way as he set off down the driveway. "I promised Paige Nichols ... we need to find out who Beanie really belongs to.... Don't, George. Please listen to me!"

But he was gone, and Ella was left with a bunch of flyers and a sinking feeling that Beanie's future had suddenly slipped out of her hands.

"What's gotten into you? You should be happy!" Caleb stood behind the desk in the reception area, ready for a face-off with Ella.

George had beaten her back to Animal Magic and had already put in his offer to give Beanie a new home. He appealed to Mom, who was studying spreadsheets on the computer. "We've got the hutch and everything. You can come and see it if you want."

"But Mom, can't we wait a few days?" Ella pleaded. She was wishing desperately that she'd found time to talk to her mom about her plan. "Does Beanie have to be adopted right away?"

Caleb stepped in on his friend's side. "Of course she does! Mom, don't listen to Ella. Beanie would love it at George's place. And he's had pet rabbits before, remember!"

"I promised Paige I'd find Beanie's real owner!" Ella told her mom. "Dad knows about it. Beanie's really shy and scared. She needs someone special."

"Hey, watch it," Caleb muttered. "Are you saying George isn't special?"

"No. I didn't mean that." Ella grew flustered. "It's just too soon. Beanie needs to stay here for a while."

"Make up your mind," Caleb snapped. "One minute you want to send her back to an owner who let her run off in the first place and couldn't care less about her anyway. The next minute, you want to keep her here!"

Sighing, Mom stood up next to her children. "Caleb, Ella, stop arguing. It's giving me a headache."

Caleb clamped his mouth shut and frowned at Ella. She took a deep breath and glared back.

"That's better." Mom came to the counter to talk to George. "It's good of you to offer Beanie a home," she began.

Yes! Caleb stared triumphantly at his sister.

"But have you checked with your mom and dad?"

Of course he hasn't! Ella gritted her teeth and kept on glaring. *He got on his bike and dashed right down here!*

"Mom won't mind," George answered steadily.

"But you haven't actually asked her yet?"

"No."

See! Ella outstared her brother.

Caleb dropped his gaze and shuffled some papers on the counter.

"What I suggest is this," Mom decided, turning to Ella and trying to soften the blow. "We have to be fair about it. I think George should go home and talk to his parents about offering Beanie a home. If they say yes, we should go ahead because we know George and we can be sure that he'll take good care of Beanie."

So who's right now? Caleb flashed Ella a final look of triumph.

Ella's heart thudded. Her shoulders sagged.

"But!" Mom held up a warning finger. "In the meantime, Ella, I suggest you keep on with your search."

Ella took a sharp breath, then nodded.

"Let's give you 24 hours to find Beanie's first owner. If by then you haven't succeeded, and if George's parents agree, we'll send her to Three Oaks Road—end of story!"

Chapter Nine

Suspicious Behavior

Never make a promise you can't keep! Annie's words ran through Ella's head as she went out to deliver more flyers.

She thought of Paige Nichols and her parents packing up all their stuff and moving away to Canada, and she worried about poor little Beanie cowering in her cage and hiding from the world.

She had a day to try to keep her promise and about 20 more houses in town to deliver to. With every click of a mailbox, she prayed that the mystery of Beanie's real owner would be solved.

"Okay?" Mom asked when Ella at last walked back into the kitchen. It was one o'clock—time for a quick break from the busy routine at Animal Magic.

"I suppose." Ella nodded.

"No luck with Beanie's original owners, I take it?"

A quick shake of the head was all Ella could manage.

"Well, look at it this way," Mom went on cheerfully. "If Beanie is given a home with George, at least you and Caleb will be able to pop in and visit her as often as you like."

"Mom, I don't want to talk about it," Ella muttered, glancing out of the kitchen window and seeing Ben

Robinson carrying Buster across the yard. "Is Joel in the reception area?" she checked.

"I'm not sure, but you can go and see," Mom replied.

Ella sped across the yard and caught up with Ben. "What's up with Buster?" she asked as she held the door open and they went inside to find Joel sitting at the desk.

"He's not eating well," Ben told her. "I tried giving him puppy food, but he wasn't interested."

"Let me take a look at him," Joel offered.

Little Buster squirmed, then wagged his tail at Joel.

"He seems lively enough. Let's take his temperature and check him over.... Yep, quite normal."

Ella watched Ben Robinson closely.
The boy's attention didn't seem to be on
Buster at all, she noticed. Instead, he
sifted through the flyers on the desk.

"Can I help?" she offered.

"No. Yes. Um, do you have a flyer on
feeding puppies?" he mumbled.

Ella got him one from the rack.

"His temperature's normal, and there's
no tenderness around his stomach," Joel
reported. "Maybe Buster is having a

slight reaction to the shot we gave him, that's all."

Ben nodded. "Oh, and do you have one of those flyers about the runaway rabbit?" he dropped in casually. But his face was bright red, and his eyes were worried.

"No, sorry, I gave away the last ones earlier this morning." *Wait a minute!* Ella thought. *Why are you so interested in Beanie? How come you snuck a look at her through the window yesterday when you thought no one would be watching?*

Ben frowned and mumbled. "Okay, no problem."

"While you're here, let me finish putting Buster's information on file," Joel suggested, turning to the computer. "We must have been too busy yesterday to take everything down."

"Age—six and a half weeks, which means Buster was born...."

"What do you know about Beanie?" Ella hissed at Ben. This time she wasn't going to let him sneak away.

"Nothing!" he said quickly. "I don't know anything!"

"Are you sure?" Ella didn't believe him. He'd answered too quickly and refused to meet her gaze.

"I said nothing—okay?" Sulkily Ben picked Buster up and turned to leave.

But Joel had one more question. "Hang on a second, Ben—where do you live? We didn't take down your address."

"We live on Ridgewood Lane," Ben answered in his usual mumble. "We just moved in."

"Ridgewood Lane," Joel typed on the keyboard. "What number?"

"23," Ben told him, escaping through the door as fast as he could.

Ella stood for a few moments gaping at the door.

"What is it?" Joel asked. "You look like you've seen a ghost."

"23 Ridgewood Lane," Ella repeated under her breath. "That's where Paige Nichols lived. The Robinsons must have moved into her house!"

"So?" Joel didn't get the point. He scratched his head and stared at Ella as she charged after Ben and overtook him at the gate.

"Wait!" she yelled.

"Leave me alone," Ben said. He brushed past Ella. "I don't want to talk to you."

"That's because you're feeling guilty," Ella guessed. "You're acting weird because of Beanie, aren't you?"

"No. Go away." Ben marched up Main Street with Buster on his leash. "I don't know what you're talking about."

"Stop!" Ella ran in front of Ben and blocked his way. "I can't quite make sense of this yet, but I've got a feeling that Beanie belongs to you!"

Ben came to a sudden halt. "Don't be silly," he argued feebly. "We just moved into our new house."

"So you've never seen Beanie before?"

He quickly shook his head and tried to barge past once more. But Ella stood her ground.

"Then how come you snuck a look at her yesterday? And why did you want

a flyer?" Ella ran through her list of suspicions. "Lastly, why pretend Buster was sick and bring him into Animal Magic?"

"I wasn't pretending," Ben faltered. Then he changed his mind. "Okay. What if I was?"

Ella stared at him long and hard. "You're either very weird, or you know something you're not telling," she accused.

Ben had run out of arguments. "What if I do?" he said huffily. "It's none of your business."

Ella seized her chance. "It is my business," she insisted.

"Okay, fine, Miss Clever! How would you feel if you had a pet and you did something you shouldn't, and it meant

that everything went wrong and you
didn't know any way of putting it right?"

"Slow down!" Ella begged. "What did
you do?"

"If I tell you, you can't tell anybody else!" Ben pleaded.

Ella nodded. "I won't."

"Mom and Dad gave me a pet rabbit when we lived at our old house on Cherry Lane, in town."

"It's near where I go to school," Ella said quickly.

"I hadn't had her very long. I named her Maisie. She was only a baby, and I hated leaving her on her own. And what I did, which I should never have done, was to sneak her into my dad's car one day without my parents knowing."

"Why?" Ella wanted to know.

"Because I thought she'd be lonely if I left her behind in her hutch, and I knew Mom and Dad would say no if I asked if we could bring her along."

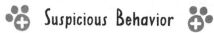

"Okay. Then what?"

"Then my dad drove us out here to Crystal Park to see the house we were moving to," Ben explained.

"Number 23 Ridgewood Lane!"

"Right," Ben said glumly. "Anyway, Mom and Dad went into the house to measure windows for curtains and stuff, and I stayed in the car with Maisie. I was playing with her and I didn't notice Mom and Dad come back."

"So Maisie was loose in the car?" Ella prompted.

Ben nodded. "Mom opened the car door and frightened Maisie and she jumped out, but Mom was too busy to notice."

"Maisie ran away?"

"Yes. And I couldn't get out and chase

her because I wasn't supposed to have her with me in the first place. Anyway, before I knew it, Dad had started the car and we were on our way."

"Then it was too late." Ella got a clear picture of what had happened. "And when you got back home, your mom and dad found the hutch was empty and thought that Maisie had escaped from your yard on Cherry Lane. You went along with it so you wouldn't get into trouble."

Miserably, Ben nodded again. "Yes, what else could I do? But then we moved here, and yesterday I saw those rabbit flyers on your counter."

"And now you want to know if Beanie is the same rabbit as the one you lost?" Ella asked, her eyes sparkling eagerly.

"Yeah. I mean, could it be Maisie? She looks the same."

"And she's a runaway. She was found in the shed at number 23." The story fit. Ella held her breath.

"I never knew that. So you think there's a good chance?" Ben asked.

"That Beanie is Maisie? Yes, I do!" Ella felt sorry and nervous—sorry for Ben, who had gotten himself into this mess, and nervous in case she was wrong. "Come on," she said, turning Ben and Buster around and heading back to Animal Magic. "There's only one way to find out. Let's go and take a closer look!"

Chapter Ten

A Perfect Match

"John Smith said yes!" Caleb stood in the rescue center doorway with bad-boy Buddy. He greeted Ella and Ben with a broad smile. "I talked to him on the phone. His girlfriend says yes, he can adopt Buddy."

"Great news!" Ella said. She patted Buddy, who wagged his stumpy tail.

"Owen's mom says she'll train Buddy to stop chewing stuff he shouldn't," Caleb went on. "She did it once before with Bruno, so she figures she can do it again."

"Sounds perfect," Ella said, hurrying on with Ben and Buster.

"Poppety-pop! Where's Neil?" Peppy the parakeet chirped from his perch.

"And we've got a woman named Emma Dade coming in to see Shadow this afternoon," Joel reported from his seat at the computer. "She already owns a brown Labrador, and she lives in a house overlooking a park where she can walk the dog, so she sounds promising."

"Good. Cool. Great," Ella rambled. "Come on, Ben, what are you waiting for?"

Ben hung back in the reception area. "I-I've changed my mind," Ben stammered.

Ella's jaw dropped. She noticed that Joel was watching Ben closely, as if he was about to step in and say something.

So she grabbed Ben by the arm and marched him through the door into the small animals unit. "Are you crazy?" she hissed. "You can't change your mind about stuff as important as this!"

Ben shook his head. "I'm going to be in big trouble with Mom and Dad if they find out," he muttered. "I mean, if Beanie turns out to be Maisie like you think—well, what am I going to tell them?"

Ella studied his frowning face. "The truth," she said matter-of-factly. "Tell them you made a mistake."

Leaving Ben to work through his problem, she approached Beanie's cage.

A Perfect Match

"Hi there!" she whispered to the shy creature huddled in the folds of her favorite blue blanket. "Someone's here to see you!"

Warily, Beanie edged forward, responding as usual to Ella's gentle voice. She twitched her soft pink nose and flicked her ears.

"I think you'll remember this person," Ella whispered. Slowly she opened the cage door and let Beanie sniff her hand. Then gently she picked her up and lifted her out.

Ben stared at Ella and Beanie. His frown disappeared and he came closer. "It's Maisie!" he said, unable to take his eyes off the tiny rabbit. "Definitely her. I'm totally sure!"

"I knew it was," Ella smiled.

The baby rabbit snuggled close against her, blinking her big dark eyes.

"Can I hold her?" Ben asked.

"Of course you can—she's your rabbit!" Taking Buster from Ben, she handed Beanie over.

"Hey, Maisie!" Ben whispered, his eyes filling with tears. "It's me—Ben!"

The rabbit sniffed his hand and hoodie. She didn't struggle or try to hide.

"She remembers you!" Ella told him. "She's not the least bit shy."

"I can't believe it," Ben muttered, holding his pet rabbit close to his chest. Then he made a big decision. "Don't worry, Maisie—whatever Mom and Dad say, I'm never going to let you go ever again!"

"So you all had a busy day," Dad said over dinner that evening.

"Caleb successfully found a home for Buddy," Mom reported. "Joel thinks he found a new owner for Shadow, and George Stevens agreed to take Lucky, the black-and-white Dutch rabbit."

"Huh?" Dad paused, fork in hand. "When I spoke to you earlier, didn't you say that George wanted to offer a home to the little white one—what's her name?"

"Beanie," Caleb told him.

"Maisie!" Ella cut in. "Her real name's Maisie, and we did what I wanted to do— we found her first owner!"

"Not so much of the 'we,'" Caleb corrected. "Ella went solo on this one." He tried to sound casual, but secretly he was impressed with his little sister.

"Ella did really well," Mom said with a smile. "The way she tracked down all the clues, I'm convinced she's going to be a detective when she's older!"

Ella glowed with pride. "The real owner's name is Ben Robinson," she told her dad. "He lives at the Nichols' old house. It's a long story."

"Lo-ong!" Caleb broke in with a
pantomime yawn. "So, Dad, you want to
know how come George took Lucky?" he
asked Dad.

"I have a feeling you're going to tell me."

"Okay, so he comes to Animal Magic
with his mom to say yes, they can give
Beanie a home. They arrive at the same
time as Mr. Robinson. It turns out Joel
had called him and asked him to come
across to Animal Magic."

"Because Joel was worried about
Ben coming in with Buster when there
was obviously nothing wrong with the
puppy," Ella cut in. This was her story
and she wanted to tell it her way. "So
Ben walks out of the small pets section
with Beanie, whose real name is Maisie,

like I said. He sees his dad, and he's shaking from head to toe."

"But it turns out that Mr. Robinson is happy that Ben found his pet rabbit at last," Caleb explained. "And when he finds out the whole truth, he doesn't throw a fit, like Ben expected."

"Whoa!" Dad put up his hands to ward off the flood of facts. "I take it that's why George offered Lucky a home—because Beanie, whose real name is Maisie, had been reunited with Ben?"

Caleb and Ella nodded.

"You should've seen Ben's face when I first handed Maisie over to him," Ella sighed. "He was so-o-o happy!"

"And Mr. Robinson said he'd buy a hutch before the pet shop in town closed, and Ben could take his long-lost baby rabbit away right then and there," Caleb said. He polished off his plate of spaghetti. "Happy ending. Then Ella almost goes and spoils it all by blubbering."

"I never did!" Ella objected. Sure, she'd been sorry to say good-bye to Beanie, and there had been tears in her eyes, but mainly she was happy for Beanie—and Lucky—and Buddy—and Shadow! Everything had worked out. "We had such a cool day!" she sighed.

🐾 🐾 🐾 🐾 🐾

"Dear Paige," Ella wrote in her email. *"This is a picture of Beanie in her new hutch. And guess what? She's living with Ben Robinson at your old house."*

Clicking the mouse to move Beanie's image onto an email attachment, Ella blew the image up to fill the screen.

Beanie–Maisie had been staring right at the phone when Ella took her picture. The photo had captured all of her best points—her little round face, her furry body, and those long silky soft ears.

"Cute!" she breathed.

"Beanie is back where she belongs like I promised," Ella wrote to Paige. *"How cool is that!"*